Richard Manning Hodges

A Memorial Address Read at the Funeral of John Angier

Shaw

Richard Manning Hodges

A Memorial Address Read at the Funeral of John Angier Shaw

ISBN/EAN: 9783337400149

Printed in Europe, USA, Canada, Australia, Japan

Cover: Foto ©Andreas Hilbeck / pixelio.de

More available books at **www.hansebooks.com**

A

MEMORIAL ADDRESS

READ AT THE FUNERAL OF

JOHN ANGIER SHAW,

IN THE MEETING HOUSE OF THE

First Congregational Society in Bridgewater,

OCTOBER 8, 1873.

BY

RICHARD M. HODGES.
\\

WITH AN APPENDIX.

CAMBRIDGE:

PRESS OF JOHN WILSON AND SON.

1874.

FUNERAL ADDRESS.

IN the circumstances under which we are
now assembled, Christian friends, it is
not in my heart to solicit your indulgence.
Ah! it is not I who speak. It is God; it is
Providence; it is the gentle Spirit of grace,
— your own best affections, if you will but
listen to their most tender accents, — each
and all of them have a distinct and emphatic
voice, here and now, in the presence of these
emblems of death and the grave.

> " While Thee I seek, protecting Power,
> Be my vain wishes stilled ;
> And may this consecrated hour
> With better hopes be filled."

It is no new occasion that excites our

deepest sympathies. Often have they been greatly moved before. Life is in the appointment of God. Death is in the appointment of God. The presence of a wise Providence is seen in them both. But in proportion to the purity and culture of our affections is the effect of them more or less forcibly felt by us. The blossom of infant life, that is just expanding and creating hopes of growth and maturity, gives to the mind and heart of a thoughtful and true parent emotions of a grateful nature, such as are only experienced by those who sustain a similar relationship. And when the grave is opened to receive the venerable form of one who was entitled to our love and rightly deserved our respect, it is impossible but that our sensibilities should be tenderly touched, for so we are graciously constituted. Jesus, our great Exemplar, wept at the grave of Lazarus. Still, life and death are alike in charge and at the disposal of the Supreme Arbiter of all events. God is equally wise and good in giving and in taking away. He is unchangeable in all his attributes, and perfect in his administration. On this thought alone can the prayer of resignation rest, "Thy will be done."

Sudden death, viewed in the light of divine Providence, is certainly not to be deprecated. Death, when it cuts down in a moment the thoughtless, the worldly-minded, the undutiful child of mortality, may well, and does indeed, in accordance with the admonitions of both natural and revealed religion, excite emotions directly opposite to those that we experience at the unlooked-for departure of the true, the faithful, the God-loving, and the man-loving friend of our hearts and brother of our humanity.

Were it to be left to our choice, however, — might we be permitted reverently to in-

dulge such a thought, — there are reasons,
seemingly meeting with the sanction of our
limited apprehension, which would cause us
to prefer that a season of calm and submissive sensibility should be granted us previous
to the moment of dissolution. How many
the words of warning and of counsel, of encouragement and of hope, that have pro-
ceeded from the lips of dying loved ones,
and which are treasured up in fond hearts!
These precious words, it cannot be doubted,
in the interposition of the Holy Spirit, are
blessed to the elevation, the purification, the
sanctification of many a soul in the kingdom
of heaven. It is this experience in the dim
light of the death-chamber that makes sacred
the memory of many a Christian parent, and
illumines recollections that might otherwise,
in the weakness of human nature, be envel-
oped in darkness, and attended with oppres-
sive influences sadly impeding the onward

and upward progress of life. The pictures and the sentiments that are engraven in devout minds of the repose and hope and joy of those who, in the Spirit of Jesus, have ceased to exist, are some of the consecrated means of grace in the consummation of the world's salvation.

A beloved man,* a true minister in the service of Christ, assisted me in my professional studies by his counsels and instructions. He held a chosen place in my heart. It pleased the Almighty Disposer of all events to appoint that his work in the cause of his Master should cease while he was yet in the morning of life. He died at the age of twenty-six years. In a quiet interval of waiting for the summons of the death-messenger, he called a younger brother to his

* John Emery Abbot was born in Exeter, N. H., on the sixth day of August, 1793. Ordained minister of the North Church in Salem, Mass., on the twentieth of April, 1815. He died on the sixth of October, 1819.

bed-side, and having presented to him a Bible, with some words of affection, said to him, "I wish you, my dear brother, to see with what composure a Christian can die." This incident in such a life has not ceased, after a period of more than fifty years, to have a sacred effect upon my mind. The incident, in all the meaning it carries with it, in the affection it discovers, in the faith it exemplifies, in the deep impression it has made upon my heart, assures me of the truth, and confirms the sustaining power, of the doctrine of immortality.

But, dear friends, we would not presume to doubt the wisdom of that decree which makes the time and manner of death unknown to us. The Giver and Preserver of life has mercifully concealed from our view the scenes of futurity. "Boast not thyself of to-morrow; for thou knowest not what a day may bring forth." It is sufficient for us

o know that God, our Father and Friend, is
he wise and righteous Author of life and
of death. Let us, in the plenitude of our
aith, and in the fulness of our hearts, say,
'Thy will be done."

Faithfully, friends of my heart, in the
gratification of my affections, and in fulfil-
ment of my office on this occasion, would I
gather up and present to you my recollections of the venerable man whose remains
are before us in the vestments of the tomb.
But I fear that my limited time and imper-
fect health will interpose obstacles to a true
and appropriate delineation of his character.
Not for his sake, oh! not for his sake would
I speak, or do I speak; but for our sakes,
beloved hearers, in the remembrance that
we also are mortal, and that the grave now
ready for these relics awaits the advent of
each of our mortal bodies.

JOHN ANGIER SHAW was a native of the South Parish of Bridgewater, now known by the corporate name of the originally extended, but at present limited, township. He was born on the eighth day of October, 1792, just eighty-one years ago to-day. In the direct line of his ancestors were men of a classical education who dedicated their powers and affections to sacred studies and duties in two of the precincts of ancient Bridgewater, and from these kindred he derived his name.* He loved, with a constant love, the home of his childhood, made venerable to him as having been the chosen seat of his worthy grandparents. He gloried, as well he might, in a residence in

---

* The Rev. John Shaw, grandfather of John Angier Shaw, was graduated at Harvard College in 1729, and ordained in South Bridgewater, 17 November, 1731. He married Ruth, the daughter of Rev. Samuel Angier, of Watertown (Har. Col., 1673), and sister of Rev. John Angier, of East Bridgewater (Har. Col., 1720). John died 29 April, 1791, aged 82. Ruth died 1768, aged 63.

the county of Plymouth, a name that brings with it the cherished association of the Pilgrim Fathers. The Pilgrim Fathers, the men who coveted, and nobly strove for, the boon of liberty, — though without a full understanding of its intrinsic value, — a liberty that should animate with a true life their own souls; a liberty which it is difficult, because of the strong principle of selfishness that pervades human nature, to preserve in its purity and to transmit unimpaired to succeeding generations. The Pilgrim Fathers, brave men! whose self-sacrificing deeds will maintain for them an honored memory in the minds and hearts of their posterity in all coming ages. I cannot but think that the love which our departed friend had for these fearless pioneers in the cause of freedom and of a popular nobility had an important effect in the formation of his own character.

Dr. Samuel Shaw,* the father of him whose obsequies we observe, it was not my privilege to know. He died before the relation which I had the happiness to hold to the First Congregational Society in Bridgewater was instituted. He was an active member of the medical profession, and lived in the respect of those who received tokens of his friendly care and the benefit of his healing art.

Mrs. Olive Leonard Shaw,† the mother of the deceased, was a friend of my early days in pastoral duty; and I loved to sit in the light of her countenance, and to receive from her the encouragement and counsel that age and wisdom imperceptibly impart to those who place themselves within their benign influences. I associate with my

* Samuel, youngest son of Rev. John and Ruth Angier Shaw, born 1750, died 4 Dec., 1819.

† Olive, daughter of Zebulon Leonard, of Middleboro', born 1755, died 3 Oct., 1837.

recollection of her the occurrence of the annual Autumnal Festival of Massachusetts, a day which invariably found me in her presence, and that of her family, with my congratulatory greetings. At that early period, Thanksgiving Day was confined to the New England States, and I believe that to some of them it was not then, as it is now, known. I trust that the influence of the day, under the cognizance and by the appointment of the general government, will work for the unity and prosperity of the entire body of our American Republic.

Mr. Shaw's preparatory education was obtained at the Bridgewater Academy. He was admitted to Harvard College in 1807, before he had quite reached the age of fifteen years. In 1811 he received the usual diploma. Of his class, which at their commencement numbered forty-nine, but nine, according to the Triennial Catalogue pub-

lished in 1872, remain among the living.
Of his classmates there were men of distinguished reputation who honored offices
in civil, literary, professional, and religious
life,—men who in honoring their duties, not
simply as duties, but as genial activities,
honored themselves. In this connection, I
am happy to say that Mr. Shaw had in rev-
erent regard his Alma Mater. He loved
to visit her halls on academic days; and the
greetings that he gave to and received from
professional gentlemen and the alumni of
the University showed, with delightful sig-
nificance, the mutual interest that was felt
in the power and progress of good learning.
At Commencement of this year, his presence was gratefully noticed by some—alas,
how few!—of his contemporaries.

After the period of his Baccalaureate
course, Mr. Shaw remained in Cambridge
under the auspices of the College, holding

the office of Regent. While a resident
graduate, he pursued the study of divinity.
There was not then, as now, a prescribed,
systematic course of theological education.
The gentlemen who were preparing for the
sacred ministry sought and received the as-
sistance and instruction of several of the
professors whose course of research and
way of thought were coincident with in-
vestigations in the science of theology. By
the help of lectures on Hebrew literature,
and the laws of Biblical interpretation, to-
gether with critical expositions of the origin,
meaning, and design of Christianity, the beginning was made of a life all whose ener-
gies and affections were to be dedicated,
under God, to the cause of truth and righteousness as instituted by Jesus Christ.

Mr. Shaw, at the proper time, received
from the local ecclesiastical association the
usual approbation to preach, and soon after-

ward, as a minister of the gospel and a school-teacher, performed the duties of both offices in Woodville, in the State of Mississippi. I have his authority for stating that in that part of the country, when he began professional life, it was thought that a minister, unless he could speak memoriter or extempore,—that is to say, without the aid of a manuscript,—was not worthy of his vocation. To meet this popular opinion, and to satisfy the demand that it imposed, Mr. Shaw was prompted to write his sermons and then commit them to memory; for he had not, to a more than ordinary degree, the gift of a free and fluent elocution. This extra labor of preparing for his pulpit services, and the loss of time that it involved, which he thought was unreasonable, if not unjustifiable, induced him to resign altogether the duties of the sacred profession, and to devote himself to the employment of teaching the young.

It is in my way here to speak, as I think
I confidently can, of the faith of him whose
funeral rites we celebrate. His faith was a
Christian faith, deriving its life and spirit
from Jesus, the revealer of truth and the in-
spirer of love. Jesus, as he apprehended him,
was the Heaven-sent messenger of grace, and
the true source of light to man as the child of
God and the heir of immortality. The mission of the Son of God, in his view, looked
directly to the enlightenment, the elevation,
the emancipation of the ignorant, the de-
graded, the sinful in the world of humanity.
He believed in " One God and Father of all,
who is above all, and through all, and in us
all." To this infinite and holy One, in humility
and submission, he bowed his spirit in worship. As he rendered worship to God, so he
gave to the Son of God the homage of his
gratitude, his obedience, and his love. How
any, in the sense of indifference or in the

mistaken sense of erudition, could virtually
or gravely declare that they were outside of
the pale of Christianity when they were
nurtured within its sacred fold, was beyond
his comprehension. As well might they
say that they were outside of the care and
influence of civilization when they were
immediately basking in the sun of its prosperity, and conscious — if submissive to the
rule of their better thoughts — that civilization itself, in its life and conduct, is indebted
to the grace and genius of Christianity. Our
departed friend received the New Testament, in its authenticity, as the revelation of
the will of God in Christ. The institutions
of the gospel, invested with a studied sense
of their meaning, were honored by him with
sentiments becoming a disciple of Christ and
a lover of righteousness. He knew the
worth and efficacy of prayer, and sought
fervently for the healthful influences of the

Holy Spirit, happy in the belief that they who ask, under a deep feeling of their need, shall receive.

Mr. Shaw had decided convictions with regard to the interpretation of divine truth, and was open and unreserved in the expression of them, as private or public opportunity demanded or favored. Still, he was no partisan in religion, in the exclusive meaning of partisanship. Oh,- no! He cared but little for the name, so that the essence was in being. " Words are the daughters of earth, and deeds are the sons of heaven." He could bow at any altar that had been consecrated to the word and work of Jesus, and could greet as a brother of mortality, and again of immortality, any one who breathed and lived in the atmosphere of a true life, a life baptized in the spirit of self-sacrifice, and of devotion to the labor of ameliorating the condition of humanity and making it wiser, purer, better, and happier. He was not ostentatious. He was rather inclined to be humble and retiring from observation. He occupied a place in society that will be vacant for a time, but which, in the providence of God, will eventually be filled. God permits no work to fail because of the want of efficient power.

Mr. Shaw, both at a distance and at home, employed his abilities in the arduous and responsible task of teaching. For several years he was preceptor of the academy in his native town, and president of the board of trustees of that seminary. He was faithful to himself and to his charge. It was his highest ambition not only to teach with fidelity, but with success. It was his unceasing desire that his pupils, in consequence of his instruction, should be self-conscious of receiving some useful knowledge. The best systems of education, as they com-

manded attention, were the objects of his
study. And the best interests of learning,
as they manifested themselves in all departments of instruction, secular and religious,
received his eager attention and his ready
support.

In connection with education, I call to
mind that Mr. Shaw had a nice perception
of the beauty of art in its relation to archi-
tecture. The plan of the Episcopal Church
in this town was the product of his pencil.
And there is extant in Christ Church, in
Cambridge, a picture drawn by him in his
undergraduate days at college, giving a
pleasing representation of the church edifice
— noted for its symmetry — and the sur-
roundings, as they appeared in the beginning
of this century.

In political life, our revered friend was
active in thought and judicious in counsel.
In the lower and higher departments of the

legislature of the Commonwealth, by general
consent, his voice was worthy to be heard
and his influence to be felt. In politics, he
was honorable and disinterested. He re-
garded the public welfare, and looked with
caution upon special or private issues. The
opinion that he held was his own, inde-
pendent of any monition he might receive
from party, or that party might be solici-
tous to give. He was consequently a good
citizen of an enlightened and liberal Republic.

In a moment, on the morning of the fourth
day of the present month, he ceased to live;
and the affections and hopes, that in their
truth and purity adorn and brighten this
earth, were withdrawn for ever.

I have sought to delineate the character
of your friend and of my friend as it presented itself to my observation. Nothing is
to be gained by a departure from the truth.

It is the truth that is to enlighten and renovate the world.

It would be neither wise nor well here and now to speak words of consolation and of sympathy to those who, by this bereavement, have been widowed and made fatherless. They know full well that the prayer of faith and of love in their behalf is offered to the widow's God and the Father of the fatherless, in obedience to that precept which enjoins that we should " bear one another's burdens, and so fulfil the law of Christ."

And now, friend of my earlier days and of my later years, fare thee well! I thank God that it was permitted me, not to speak thy praises, but of the worth of life as it was in thy heart to represent it. Thou hast gone before me to thine eternal home. Yet a little while longer, and the gates, that have been opened so unexpectedly to receive thee, will be opened to receive me

to the home in which life will be uninter-
rupted, and the life of God in the soul be
for ever lived!

Friends! fellow-travellers to the world
beyond the grave! ye for whom the beloved
Son of God lived, and for whom he died!
let this scene and this service have a pos-
itive and present meaning to each one of
you. They indeed have a meaning which,
if understood by you, will elevate and
hallow all your conceptions of life. They
will teach you to sing, as the poet, with
regenerating power, has sung:—

> " Life is real, life is earnest,
> And the grave is not its goal;
> ' Dust thou art, to dust returnest,'
> Was not spoken of the soul."

If this language is tuned to notes of high
aspiration, how much grander and more
ennobling is the language of inspiration,
" I am the resurrection and the life: he

that believeth in me, though he were dead, yet shall he live : and whosoever liveth, and believeth in me, shall never die " !

Friends, may God bless you ! May God bless each one of you! May the Holy Spirit bless my word! Amen.

APPENDIX.

I.

THE Rev. GEO. HERBERT HOSMER, the friend and pastor of Mr. SHAW, has recorded the following testimony to his upright and useful life, in the "Christian Register" of the 18th of October, 1873 : —

In Bridgewater, 4th inst., Hon. JOHN ANGIER SHAW, eighty-one years.

"Like as a shock of corn cometh in his season," so, full of glorious fruitage, our brother passes on to the deep, pure life of heaven.

Sudden departures are sometimes glorious translations. In the peace of the early morning, with bright waking thoughts in his mind, sweet words on his lips, and the sunlight of earth breaking upon his eyes, he bowed his head, and suddenly the sunlight of heaven broke upon his vision, — no pain, no anxiety, scarcely a flutter of the spirit's wings was heard, — only serene, grateful peace.

Born in Bridgewater, Oct. 8, 1792, he gave proof of his ability and diligent application by entering Harvard College at an unusually early age, and was graduated with honor in the class of 1811, remarkable for its men of eminent talents. He fitted for the ministry, and entered upon the work, but relinquished it after a brief period. He was called to the South, where he devoted himself to teaching; and, after a few years' residence in Mississippi, returned to Bridgewater, and took charge of the academy for a period extending over sixteen years.

He was called to serve this community in the different branches of the State Legislature, first as Senator for two years, then as Representative for four years, holding these offices with honor, and discharging their duties with conscientious fidelity.

In the year 1841, under the recommendation of Horace Mann, he was called to New Orleans to organize and superintend the public school system of that city, on which work he entered with great earnestness, and achieved an enviable success. To this day his services are gratefully remembered by the citizens of that place. After about ten years of labor in laying the foundation of a system of popular education at the South, he returned to Bridgewater, where he has resided the greater part of the time since, studiously devoting himself to labors for the good of his fellowmen. To the last he was occupied in his favorite work of teaching; and, even as late as the day before his death, was engaged with his evening class of young men. For the work of an educator he was eminently fitted, and, though faithful in all he undertook, in this sphere he will be most gratefully remembered.

While a strongly pronounced conservative Unitarian, he was charitable in his spirit to all phases of Christianity, and rejoiced in the hope of a spread of a wider unity of spirit, of which he was careful to note every cheering sign. He was a constant supporter of public worship, a just and discriminating listener, and a faithful follower of Jesus Christ.

He retained his mental vigor to the last, and spent much of his time in the critical study of the New Testament, and in reading with interest the new books on the various phases of religious thought.

He took great interest in the religious instruction of the young, laboring in the Sunday school with characteristic earnestness for many years.

He stood among us a pillar of strength, remarkable for his honest frankness, purity of heart, and sincerity of spirit. In his sudden departure, this community and society lose their strongest mind, as well as a sincere, upright, pure-minded Christian gentleman.

II.

THE following memorial was published in the "North Bridgewater Gazette," November 9, 1873. J. E. CRANE, Esq., a fellow-townsman of Mr. SHAW, is the author of it : —

BRIDGEWATER.

This community was surprised on Saturday morning, the 4th inst., by the announcement of the death of Hon. JOHN A. SHAW, which occurred at an early hour at his residence, of paralysis of the heart. Mr. Shaw was born in the house where he died, Oct. 8, 1792, and was but little short of eighty-one years of age. He was the son of Dr. Samuel Shaw, and grandson of Rev. John Shaw, the second pastor of the First Congregational Church in Bridgewater. Early in youth he disclosed talents of a superior order, and was fitted for college, and entered Harvard with Edward Everett, Nathaniel Frothingham, John C. Gray, and Harrison Gray Otis, graduating in 1811. In the choice of a profession his religious cast of mind led him to a theological course, which was completed; but he subsequently relinquished it for the profession of teacher.

He went to Mississippi, where his success gave him a
high reputation; and, after remaining there several
years, was called to the preceptorship of the Bridgewater Academy in 1825. His success here is too well
known to require any extended notice, as his long connection with the academy as preceptor and president
of the board of trustees formed a very important part
of its history. His entire connection as preceptor, in
point of time, was sixteen years, terminating in 1841.
For many years he was a member of the Board of
Trustees, and at his death held the office of President
of that body. As has been already stated, it was not
here alone that he acquired celebrity as a teacher; but
at Andover, and in charge of the public schools in
New Orleans, his success was alike manifest. His just
measure of the importance of a liberal education was
ever manifest, and his testimony always emphatic
upon that point. His interest in public affairs was not
circumscribed to the school-room, but his broad culture
fitted him for other fields of usefulness. As early as
1834, his election to the State Senate was evidence of
the estimation in which he was held in this region;
and his subsequent election to that office in 1835, and
also four elections to the House of Representatives by
the citizens of this town, indicated his popularity as a
legislator. In both branches of the legislature he was
distinguished for his deep interest in the cause of
popular education, and was also active in originating
the measure for the reduction of the number of repre-

sentatives, which at that time had become burdensome and unwieldy. In all the walks of social life he was endeared to those with whom he was associated, as a man of great purity of heart, exerting a most beneficent influence upon all about him. Early in life he connected himself with the church of his fathers, and was a consistent example of the religion he professed. The long catalogue of those who were his pupils would show the names of many persons of eminence in the different learned professions, and his memory will be long held by them as a public benefactor. This town, from which no allurements of station could estrange him, will hold him in grateful remembrance. The institution of learning here, with which he was so closely connected, will most indelibly inscribe his name as chief among its friends, and cherish it as an important page in its history. Of an honored ancestry, he leaves a name alike honored. A widow, four daughters, and a son mourn the departure of one whose life was tenderly devoted to their welfare. The funeral obsequies were attended, on Wednesday afternoon, by a large number, at the church where, on the last Sabbath of his life, Mr. Shaw was an attentive listener, Rev. Mr. Hosmer officiating.

III.

THE annexed notice is transcribed from the
" Liberal Christian," of New York, published
25th October, 1873 :—

JOHN ANGIER SHAW.

It is fitting that a tribute of respect to the memory
of this true and venerable man should find a place in
the columns of the " Liberal Christian." He was a
faithful member of that fellowship in the ecclesiastical
world which hears reverently and receives implicitly
the teachings of the Master as the Messiah, and with
the whole heart welcomes the principles of freedom,
fraternity, and benevolence. Wherever the gospel,
in its simplicity and tenderness, in its beauty and
power, was reflected, there his best affections found
opportunity for exercise, and constant increase of
strength. He sought continually that the spirit of
his religion should be baptized with the water that
comes from " a well springing up into everlasting
life."

Mr. Shaw was graduated at Harvard College in

1811, before he had attained to the full age of nineteen. After receiving the honors of his Alma Mater, he continued to reside in Cambridge, holding the office of Registrar in the government of the University, and at the same time, with such facilities as presented themselves, pursuing the studies and meditations that lead to a preparation of the mind and heart for the work of the Christian ministry. In the process of time, having obtained the usual credentials, he went, by invitation, to the distant State of Mississippi, to exercise the pastoral office, and also to fulfil the duties of a schoolteacher. He, however, soon found it incompatible with a proper regard for the health not only of mind, but also of body, to devote his strength and thoughts to both of these important vocations. There were also certain adventitious requirements in the public conduct of the sacred office, at that period and in that remote locality, that made the weekly preparation for the pulpit on the Lord's day irksome to him. Following the guidance of what he deemed an overruling Providence, the interests of education commanded the entire exercise of his abilities. At New Orleans, in Louisiana, at the instance of a prominent educator of Massachusetts (Mr. Mann), he filled for many years the office of superintendent of the schools in that great city; and the influence of his theoretical and practical instructions in the direction of mental and physical culture is felt and acknowledged even to this day.

In Andover and Bridgewater — towns of his native State — his fidelity as a teacher has been proved; and, during an active life of guiding and disciplining growing minds, he secured to himself the grateful reward of the love of many hearts, and now that his life is ended his memory will command the tribute of a wide-spread respect and honor.

He who is the subject of our affectionate recollections was repeatedly honored with a seat in the Senate and House of Representatives of his beloved Commonwealth. His views of government were broad and generous, and his interests in the causes of good learning and civil polity were coextensive with the efficiency of a liberal education and a true religion.

All the institutions of Christianity were ever held by him in reverential regard. The Sunday school had in him a warm friend and an energetic and useful superintendent and teacher. The meetings of our Conferences, and in general the objects of the Unitarian Association, were cheered by his presence and supported by his word. He honored life by honoring himself, his powers and opportunities, his aspirations and hopes.

In the midst of life, while apparently in full health, the angel of death came to him, all unawares, with his summons to enter the spirit-land. On the morning of the 4th of this month, ere yet the sun had given evidence of his brightness, and while words of kindly

feeling were proceeding from the lips of the uncon-
sciously expiring man, his heart, paralyzed, at once
ceased from its pulsations, and the light of his earthly
life was for ever extinguished.

His funeral was attended with every expression of
respect, on Wednesday, the 8th inst., that day being
the eighty-first anniversary of his birth. The meeting-
house of the First Congregational Society in Bridgewater, where, in health, he was a constant and devout
worshipper, was filled with sympathizing friends.
The services began with a dirge by the choir. An
invocation was made, and select texts from the Scrip-
tures were read by the present pastor of the society,
Rev. Geo. Herbert Hosmer. A memorial address was
delivered by Rev. R. M. Hodges, a former pastor, and
an early and a late friend of the deceased. A concise
and appropriate sermon, from Proverbs xii. 28, was
preached by the stated minister; and the funeral prayer
was offered by Rev. George W. Hosmer, D.D. The
exercises were varied with happy effect by hymns of
consoling and quickening power.

At the grave, in the beautiful cemetery of the town,
the words of committal — "earth to earth" — were
spoken, and the insignia of death and decay were for
ever removed from mortal sight.

> Servant of God, well done;
>   Rest from thy loved employ:.
> The battle fought, the victory won,
>   Enter thy Master's joy.

39

Soldier of Christ, well done ;
Praise be thy new employ ;
And while eternal ages run,
Rest in thy Saviour's joy.

R. M. H.

CAMBRIDGE, *October* 12, 1873.

IV.

For aid in collecting the following statistics, thanks are specially due to the Hon. Artemas Hale, the oldest ex-member of Congress, who still bears his accumulated years and abundant honors with grace and dignity. "*Serus in cœlo redeat.*"

Mr. Shaw's educational and religious mission began in December, 1818. His journey to Mississippi, though relieved and cheered by the company of his sister (Mrs. Ames), was long and tedious. The facilities of travel and correspondence were not developed then as they are now. His interest in the profession of teaching, to which he now consecrated his life, prompted him to continue his work among the remote people who had at first called his attention and secured his affections in their behalf as a teacher. With the exception of one or two intervals of recreation spent at his early home, and with his friends in Massachusetts, he remained abroad for a period of nearly twenty-six years. From 1825 to 1830, and again from 1832 to 1841, he had charge of the Bridgewater Academy.

From 1841 to 1851, with the reservation of short vaca-
tions in the summer seasons, he was engaged at New
Orleans in systematizing the school department of that
city. Since his return from Louisiana, his residence
has been for the most part in Bridgewater, and his
occupation the familiar and favorite one of training
and enlightening young minds.

By the favor of his political friends in the county of
Plymouth, he was, in 1835 and again in 1838, elected
to a seat in the Senate of Massachusetts. In this high
position his influence and learning in regard to educational interests were felt and acknowledged. In token
of the confidence of his fellow-townsmen in his in-
tegrity and honor, he was chosen, for three years, —
from 1839 to 1841, inclusive, — to represent them in
the popular branch of the legislature. His fidelity to
the trust was marked by the generous and enlightened
spirit of philanthropy.

V.

FAMILY REGISTER.

JOHN A. SHAW, on the 29th March, 1821, was married, in Woodville, Miss., to Sarah Hart (Rogers) White. The children of this marriage were Olive Rosalie and Margaret Maria. Olive (Mrs. David Perkins) is living, a widow, in charge of a family. Margaret died April 10th, 1868, at the age of forty-four years. Mrs. Sarah H. Shaw died in Mississippi, 8th of May, 1824.

Mr. Shaw's second marriage was to Mira (Sprague) Washburn, on the 17th of October, 1830. There were six children by this marriage, four of whom are living, — three daughters and one son, — two daughters in matrimony. A daughter and a son died in infancy. Mrs. Shaw still resides in the honored homestead.

VI.

MR. SHAW, not infrequently, through the public press, uttered his best thoughts on subjects of immediate interest in social, literary, and religious life. His published discourses are : —

Eulogy on John Adams and Thomas Jefferson, delivered August 2, 1826, by request of the Inhabitants of Bridgewater.

An Address delivered before the Bridgewater Society for the Promotion of Temperance, February 22, 1828.

An Oration delivered before the Citizens of Plymouth, July 4, 1828, "On the Permanency of the Political System of America."

An Address delivered before the Public Schools of the city of New Orleans, February 22, 1850.

VII.

THE following paragraph from the " Eulogy "
has a meaning of permanent value : —

Hail, happy period! when civil liberty, joined with
Christian faith, shall emancipate the world from the
fetters of despotism and the galling chains of sin.
Freedom must rest on the basis of public information
and public virtue. This proposition, though often
repeated, is no oftener advanced than its obvious
importance requires. And what so efficacious as the
sanctions of eternal truth, as that light from above,
which gilds alike the lowly roof and vaulted dome, to
animate, to cheer, to purify, and guide us in the way
of virtue, peace, and equal rights? The politician
may rear his well-proportioned fabric ; but unless the
light of Christianity be there, unless its purifying spirit
shed around its holy power, degeneracy and corrup-
tion will sap the foundation. Not that it interferes
with forms of government, for its kingdom is not of
this world. Its powerful influence is a moral influence.
It designs no reforms but those of personal character.
It exalts a people only by its power on the hearts of

those who compose it. In proportion as pure Christianity prevails, — I mean the religion taught by Christ, — in proportion as divine philosophy prevails, man will respect the rights of his brother man, and be ready to obey the easy rule of liberty and love. The Christian raises in his mind no structure of the future happiness and glory of the world, without resting it on the firm and broad foundation of gospel truth. He who is the servant of sin cannot be the Lord's freeman, and he is as little qualified to be a good citizen of a free republic. A corrupt community must ere long be an enslaved community.

Cambridge: Press of John Wilson and Son.